Road Signs

Written by
Stephen Rickard

Here are some road signs.

Road signs help people in cars to be safe.

Some road signs tell the driver what he or she **must not** do.

A sign with a red circle tells you that you must not do something.

This sign means that you must not turn left.

This sign means 'no buses'.

Road signs in a blue circle tell you that you **must** do something.

This sign means you must turn right.

This sign means you must go to the left.

Road signs in a triangle give the driver a warning.

This sign warns the driver that the car could skid. The road could be wet or icy.

This sign warns the driver that there are sharp bends on the road ahead.

These road signs are from four different countries. The signs look the same.

If you are driving in a different country, you can still understand the road signs.

This helps to keep everybody safe.

The number on the sign tells the driver how fast he or she can go.

The driver **must not** drive faster than the speed on the sign.

Straßen-
schäden
40

70
RAPPEL

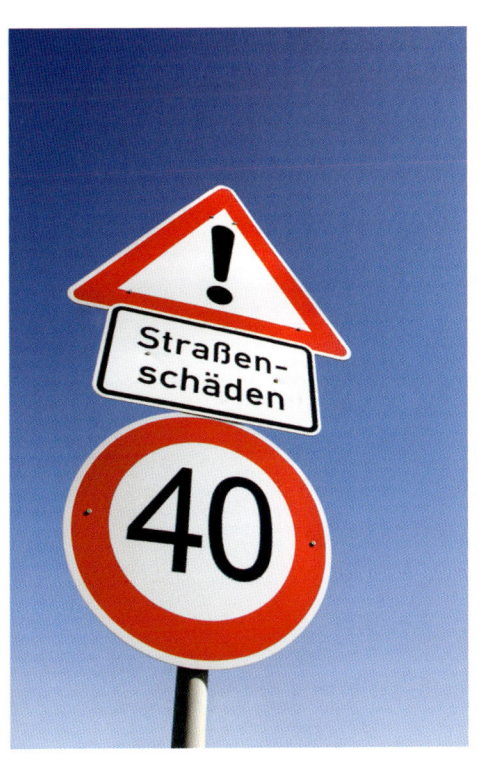

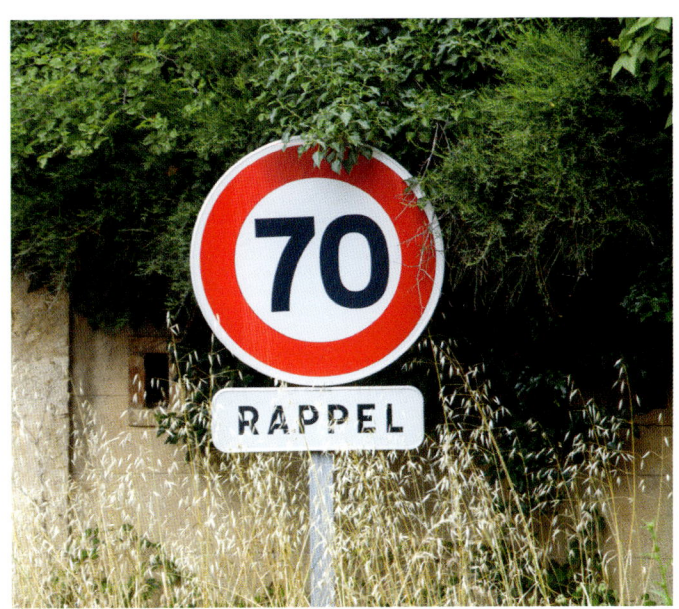

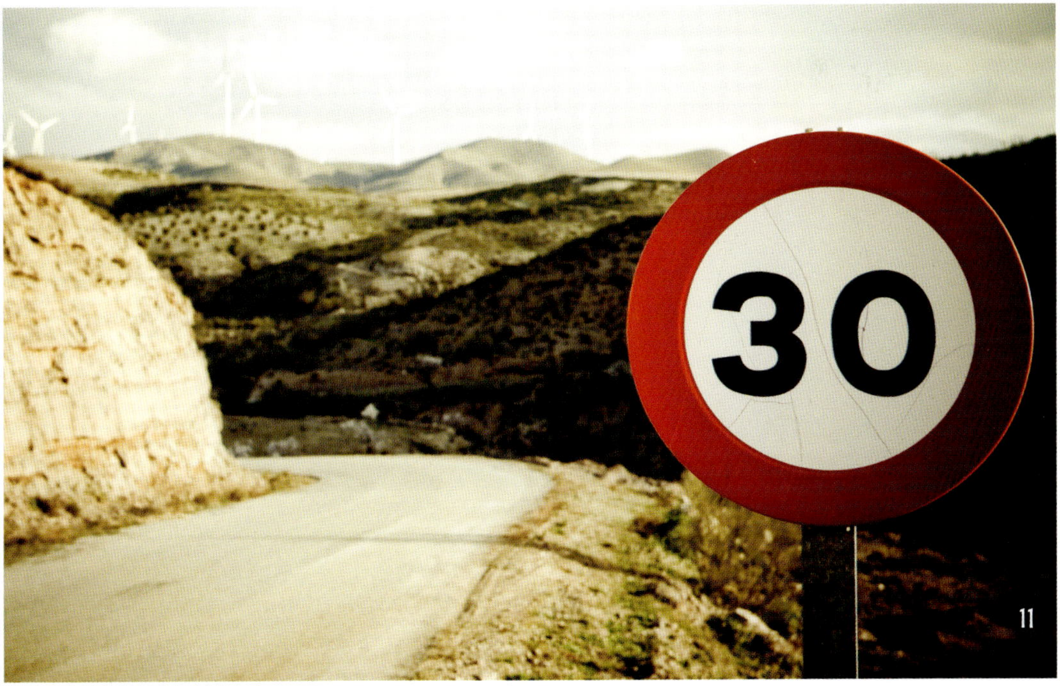
30

Many road signs have no words. They just have pictures. The picture tells you what the sign means.

It is easy for a driver to see a picture on a sign. It is harder for a driver to read words on a sign.

But the picture on the sign must be easy to understand.

These road signs are from around the world. They are all different, but it is clear what they mean.

Some road signs warn drivers about animals. The animals might be on the road.

This sign is from Australia.

This sign is from Norway.

Road signs help to keep people and animals safe.